Three Good Things

Lois Peterson

Orca currents

ORCA BOOK PUBLISHERS

Library and Archives Canada Cataloguing in Publication

Peterson, Lois J., 1952–, author
Three good things / Lois J. Peterson.
(Orca currents)

Issued in print and electronic formats.
ISBN 978-1-4598-0985-7 (pbk.).—ISBN 978-1-4598-0987-1 (pdf).—
ISBN 978-1-4598-0988-8 (epub)

I. Title. II. Series: Orca currents
PS8631.E832T47 2015   jc813'.6   C2015-901728-9
C2015-901729-7

First published in the United States, 2015
Library of Congress Control Number: 2015935530

Summary: Fifteen-year-old Leni copes with a mother who suffers
from mental illness.

MIX
Paper from
responsible sources
FSC® C016245
www.fsc.org

*Orca Book Publishers is dedicated to preserving the environment and has
printed this book on Forest Stewardship Council® certified paper.*

Orca Book Publishers gratefully acknowledges the support for its
publishing programs provided by the following agencies: the Government of
Canada through the Canada Book Fund and the Canada Council for the Arts,
and the Province of British Columbia through the BC Arts Council
and the Book Publishing Tax Credit.

Cover photography by Getty Images
Author photo by E. Henry

ORCA BOOK PUBLISHERS
www.orcabook.com

Printed and bound in Canada.

18 17 16 15 • 4 3 2 1

For my Sunday writing group,
Tony, Danika, Chris and Esther, who wer
there at the beginning of the story.

Chapter One

"Get up, Leni."

"Go away." I groan and roll over.

"Leni." Mom tugs on my covers.

I yank them away. "Not now. Not again."

It's dark under here, so dark that for a moment I don't have a clue where I am. I could be anywhere or nowhere, something or nothing.

My mother crashes around the room, muttering under her breath. I hold mine. Maybe she will forget about me, forget about whatever is on her mind, whatever has her going at whatever time this is.

Mom drags my quilt off me. "Come on. We've got to get out of here."

This scenario plays out so often I should be used to it by now. It doesn't matter if we're leaving something behind or headed somewhere specific. It's all in my mother's head.

"It's the middle of the night," I say, as if it makes a difference to her. "I'm tired."

She holds out my sweater. My shoes. "Get going."

I haul the covers back over my head.

I hear my runners thud as they hit the floor. "Fine then," she says. "I'll go without you."

I lie still. I feel Mom next to my bed. Hear her breath. "Go on then, why don't you," I mutter.

She doesn't move.

I feel my blood pulsing in my ears.

"Okay. I'm going," she says. But she still doesn't move.

How many times have we been through this stupid song and dance? Testing each other?

She wants to leave. I want to stay. Even if this place is no better than any of the others.

"Fine." She walks away. A drawer opens and closes. A chair squeals. A zipper hisses.

I can see it all, the way she pulls together the few things that have been spread around the place since we got here—one day ago, or three—into her old blue duffel bag. Shoves her bulging purse under her arm, drags her red quilt from the couch or cot she's been sleeping on this time.

Now she's standing at the door, looking back. Checking for whatever she may have left behind.

As I wait her out, my breath moves up my chest into my throat.

When I can take the silence no longer, I peer over the top of my quilt. Mom is staring at me. Not challenging or demanding. Pleading. "Leni. Come on. Please." Her hair is unbrushed. One side of her collar sticks up against her neck.

"Jeez!" I swing my legs over the side of the bed.

The one thing in the world worse than being dragged around by a crazy mom? If she left without me.

"What is it this time?" I pull on my clothes, shove my stuff into my backpack and grab my pillow and comforter, the box of cereal and two apples.

"Get moving," she says. "I'll tell you in the car."

Chapter Two

"The lottery?" I stretch out on the backseat. "You drag me out of bed in the middle of the night because you won the lottery?"

"Not me. We. What's mine is yours," she says as she turns the car onto the street.

"Of course it is." I punch my pillow and jam it under my head.

"Once word gets out, we'll get no peace." The car swerves as she turns to glare at me. "You better not tell anyone."

"Look where you're going!"

Any other person might want to know how much we had won. When we'd get the money.

What she planned to spend it on.

I'd get more sense out of her if I asked her the meaning of life.

I have asked more than once why we can't just live with my grandfather. All together. Like normal people. "If you have to ask, you're dumber than I think you are." Mom doesn't mean to be cruel. It's just that she can't always censor what comes out of her mouth. *Who knows what your grandfather's second-hand smoke will do to my hair and skin*, she said the last time I brought it up.

And when I asked Grand, he would sigh and say, *Oh, pet. It wouldn't work. It just wouldn't.*"

His house is small and dark, with fake wood panels on the walls. The furniture and carpet are all some combination of mustard yellow and olive green, steeped in cigarette smoke. We've never lived there. But it's the only place I think of as home.

I drag my comforter over me and turn my face into the back of the seat. It will be another long night of driving through the dark.

I don't know how much later it is when I'm woken by the car stopping. "Where are we?" It's barely light out.

"I'm going for coffee." Mom gets out and slams the door.

I clear the foggy window with my sleeve. We're parked tight against a chain-link fence. I loosen my tangled clothes and wipe my face with my collar. My mouth tastes like a cat died in it.

I pull out my phone.

Grand answers on the fourth ring. "That you, Leni?"

"She's done it again," I tell him.

"Which is it this time?" He sounds tired. "Got into a fight over nothing? Or left town?"

"She's taken off. We've taken off."

"Where are you?" I can hear the rattle of his coffeepot. I imagine him shuffling around in his plaid housecoat, his veined feet shoved into old leather slippers.

"In an alley."

"But where?"

"I have no idea, Grand. We drove. I fell asleep. I just woke up."

"Let me talk to her."

"She's gone for coffee."

"Ah." I hear the longing in his voice. His coffee must have perked by now, burping bubbles into the glass lid of his old pot.

"You go have your breakfast. I'll get back to you when I know where we are."

"Good girl. Before you go…what set her off this time?"

"She's won the lottery."

His bark could be laughter or disgust. "Seen the ticket, have you?"

"I haven't, no."

"Call me when you find it."

"Then what?"

He sighs. "I don't know, pet. I really don't. But call me. I worry. You know I do." He hangs up.

That's been his line for as long as I can remember. *I worry. You know I do.*

This time I want to say, *So why don't you do something about it? Why is it me who has to go along with my mother's crazy comings and goings? Put up with her highs and lows? Make sure she eats? Takes her meds?*

I imagine him at the kitchen table, slurping coffee, scrubbing at his unshaven cheeks, pulling yesterday's paper toward him.

And hear his voice saying, *It wouldn't work. It just wouldn't.* He does what he can, I guess. Always wants to know where we are, if things are okay. Tops up the bank account when it's getting low. Pays for my pay-as-you-go cell phone.

He pays and we go. That is how it works.

Mom comes back with coffee as I'm shaking out my comforter. "Take one." She holds out the cardboard tray. "I got you two honeys." She thrusts out her hip so I can grab the little packets from her pocket. She read somewhere that honey is better than sugar.

"There's nothing to stir it with."

"Use your imagination."

"Initiative, I think you mean." She can't see the look I give her.

The car is too close to the fence for me to open the front passenger door, so I climb into the back again. I root through the mess on the floor for something to stir my coffee with. All I come up with is a red-and-white-striped straw. "Where's the ticket, Mom?" I ask.

"What ticket?"

"The lottery ticket that is going to make us the envy of all. And the target of every salesperson on the planet."

"Somewhere safe."

Her purse is leaning against the passenger door. "In here?" I reach for it.

"You know a lady's purse is private." As she yanks it away from me, it flies back and hits her shoulder. "Now you've made me spill my coffee!" She dabs at her pants with a tissue.

"Where are we?" I ask.

"Richmond somewhere."

"Richmond? It took all night to get just this far?"

"I made a few detours to throw everyone off the scent. Stopped when the gas light came on."

"What time is it?"

"Time you figured out not to nag me before I've had breakfast."

I pull my comforter around my shoulders and close my eyes. "Wake me when you're done. I need a bathroom."

Mom can sleep anywhere. Everywhere. But I can't. The car gets colder and colder, and the windows get more and more fogged up. Next time I look, she is asleep with her mouth open, her empty coffee cup lying in her lap. Her purse bulges open beside her. I ease it toward me an inch at a time. When I have it in my lap, I tent my comforter over me to muffle any noise I might make.

I read somewhere that you can tell a lot about a woman's life by what's in her purse.

Mom's is stuffed with her med bottles, a dozen empty vitamin bottles and a handful of full ones. She's collected a bunch of tiny fast-food salt and pepper packages. Flyers about high-interest accounts. Credit-card applications. A reminder note for a doctor's appointment I doubt she kept. A stuffed green elephant she found under a park bench. A single sock I've never seen before.

In her wallet is a five-dollar bill, more salt and pepper packages, a photo of me perched on my dad's shoulders when I was about four, eighty-five cents in change and a little sachet of parsley seeds. Ah yes. Let's plant a garden!

But, of course, no lottery ticket.

No doubt another of her many delusions.

Chapter Three

I slide the purse back where I found it, drape the comforter over Mom and get out of the car.

This alley is no different than any other. A stack of lumber leans against two recycling cans with beat-up lids. A dead plant falling out of a wire basket lies next to a patch of oil.

I zip up my jacket and start walking.

On the next block is a big park. It has a kiddie area with three swings, a jungle gym and a slide. And a bench dedicated "To June and Matthew Long, who loved this place."

Parks are Mom's favorite hangout too, wherever we are. It may be a throwback to when she was little. Or when I was. I once told her she should write a book about urban parks. *Do I look like Danielle Steel?* was all she said.

Although the swing is pretty small, I wedge myself in. "Push me," I say aloud. "As high as the sky." Then I look around to make sure no one heard me. Everyone knows only crazy people talk to themselves.

The park is part of a community center. There's a library and an arts center and a recreation center with an arena. In the parking lot, dads are hauling kids and huge hockey bags out of cars.

I pump so hard, I am soon high enough to catch glimpses of a long highway with a gas station on almost every block. Behind a mini mall where Mom probably got the coffee stretch tidy blocks of houses surrounded by brick walls and high shrubs.

What it would be like to pump so high the swing cleared the top bar? Scary. Exhilarating. Dangerous.

Talking to yourself and risk-taking activities are two signs of mental illness. I read all about them once in a pamphlet in the waiting room of a doctor's office while Mom ranted at the doctor in an examination room.

Will knowing what symptoms to look out for keep me sane? Or send me around the bend?

I jump off the swing at its highest point, barely keeping my balance when I hit the ground.

A woman is unlocking the library when I get there. She steps aside for me to enter. "There's always an early bird or two," she says.

Another librarian sits staring at her screen. "Can I help you?" she asks without looking up.

"I'd like to use the computer," I say.

"We have two in the back corner." She smiles up at me now. "First come, first served. You'll need a library card."

"I'm just visiting." I know how this works. "Can I get a pass?"

She hands me a slip of paper. "Log in with this number."

Grand's father bought him a set of *World Book* encyclopedia when Grand was eight. He says it took him more than five years to study every entry from *A* to *Z*. That it taught him every-thing he knows. How a cow's stomach works. The weight of the Eiffel Tower.

Who hit the most runs in the 1926 baseball season. All very useful.

But when I tried to explain Wikipedia to him, he shook me off. "Too high-tech for this old geezer."

I'll probably be stuck on the *A*s forever. Today I'm reading about anthrax when someone sits down at the station next to me.

First I take no notice. When I do glance over, I nearly fall off my chair. "What the heck is that?" Beady eyes stare at me from the opening of a boy's jacket.

"Never seen a ferret before?" He pulls the creature out like it's a scarf. The ferret dangles from his hands, blinking at me.

"Not this close."

"Want to pet him?" He holds the thing out to me. "He's quite friendly."

"You gotta be kidding." I pull away. "It's a rodent!"

"Ferrets are not rodents."

"Sure they are."

He points at my screen. "Look it up if you don't believe me."

I only need to read a few lines. "Okay. So it's not a rodent. You still shouldn't be dragging it around in your coat. It's a wild creature. It needs to be free."

"Bandit would get eaten alive in the big wide world."

"Bandit?" It's got a cute little face with black markings around its eyes.

"My sister Steph wanted me to change it to Fluffy." He grins and tips back his head as Bandit burrows under his chin. He's skinny, with sandy hair and sandy skin and the palest eyes I've ever seen.

"So do you keep it in a little cage with a little wheel to run on and a little bottle to drink out of?" I don't know why I'm having this discussion with this boy.

"Bandit has a cage with a long run. Ferrets need space," he tells me. "But I daren't let him loose too often. Or everyone would be walking around barefoot." He holds out his leg to show me the chewed-up sole of his runner. "He's got a shoe fetish."

I tuck my feet under my chair. These are my only shoes. "I never had a pet," I tell him. "But if I did, it wouldn't be that."

"I've got others. But Bandit is my favorite. "

"Don't tell me you've got mice in your pockets, hamsters up your sleeves?"

"Not here. At home. I have thirty-one in my menagerie. All kinds."

"Thirty-one? Don't you need a license or something?"

"Nah. I keep them in the garage. For my twelfth birthday, Dad cleared it out and helped me make cages. Now he keeps his car in the driveway."

The last thing I got from my father was a ten-dollar movie card in the mail.

That isn't even enough for popcorn with the movie.

"Want to come over and see?" the boy asks. "I've got a pair of albino rabbits. All girls love rabbits."

How many girls? I wonder.

I'm not much of an animal lover. I've seen rats in alleys. A dead cat under a bed. Too many mean dogs.

"Well?" the boy asks.

Before I can answer, a man appears at my side. "You using that? Or can I get on?"

I look at the boy, then back at my screen. "Yes, I am using it."

"What about you?" the man asks Bandit's owner.

"It's all yours." When he gets up, he keeps one hand on his stomach. A bump there shows where the ferret has settled. Either that or this kid's got a huge tumor.

"I'm Jake, by the way." He puts out his spare hand.

What kid our age shakes hands? And who knows what kind of deadly animal germs he's carrying around on his skin?

"I've got to get back to work." Better be prepared for when the next anthrax scare happens.

"Maybe I'll see you around." He blushes. "And your name is?"

"It's Leni." I keep my hands on the keyboard.

"See you around, Leni."

I don't watch him walk away. But I hear every step, then the door opening and closing behind him.

It turns out that ferrets are in the *Mustelidae* family. Also known as the weasel family. Even rodents or weasels have to be easier to understand than people, I figure.

The man at the next computer is on a dating site. I imagine how he might describe himself. *Overweight, middle-aged man with body odor wishes to meet soul mate*. Good luck with that, I think. Then I catch myself and cringe. He's probably another lonely schmuck.

I check Craigslist for rental listings before I log off and then grab a copy of *Country Living* from the magazine rack. I turn to the ads for stainless-steel plumbing and Irish linen towels. Wrought-iron hardware and blown-glass lamps. After Dad left and Mom started moving us from place to place, I filled a scrapbook with details of the house I want one day. I picked paint colors, drapes, throw rugs and end tables.

The scrapbook got left behind in some dump we stayed in.

Whenever I open one of these home-decorating magazines, I feel a worm of envy in my gut.

For everyone else's life.

Chapter Four

When I get back to the car, Mom is still fast asleep. She has moved into the back, so I climb into the driver's seat and slam the door closed. I punch the buttons on the radio.

"Shut up," Mom mumbles.

"Did I wake you?"

"I've been waiting for you." She pulls herself up. A red crease runs down one cheek.

"There's a washroom in the park," I tell her. "But I think it's locked."

"There's a park?" Her eyes light up. "Where have you been?"

"At the library."

"A bit of knowledge is a dangerous thing. Did you know that?"

"I have to get an education somehow." I pretend to resent the fact that it's been years since I've really been in school. In truth, the thought of going to school scares the crap out of me.

Her gaze slides away from me, then back again. "So what did you learn today?" She's switched to her This-is-the-kind-of-mother-I-wish-I-was voice. Bright and expectant. But she can't keep it up. "No chance you found us somewhere to stay for the night, I suppose. Somewhere we can at least get a shower."

"Actually, there's a motel a few blocks away." I read the scribble on my arm. "The Lion Inn. Sixty-seven dollars a night."

"We could probably get a discount for a long stay. I'm behind on my shows."

"How long are you thinking?" I ask. Jake may not be cute exactly. But he did invite me to his place. Not that we ever stay in one place long enough to get to know anyone.

Mom untangles herself from the comforter and slips her purse over her shoulder. She gets out and adjusts her jacket so it's now really crooked. "As long as we need. Your Grand wouldn't want us out in the cold."

I sometimes wonder if she has any idea how much things cost. All she has to do is put a card in a hole in the wall, and money pops out. Grand makes sure there's always enough in the account, tops up our welfare check when the account gets low.

I don't know where I learned about remittance men. They were disgraced family members sent from England to the colonies, financed by the families who were glad to see the back of them. Is that how Grand thinks of her? Us?

"Come on," says Mom. "I need more coffee. Then we'll check out the motel."

Of course, nothing is that straightforward. First she makes a scene at Timmy's. She wants a Roll Up the Rim cup—that deal has been over for weeks. Then she can't find the scrap from a winning cup that entitles her to a free coffee. She empties her pockets right there on the counter. When a tampon rolls across the floor, I pretend I'm not with her. Something I've gotten good at.

Mom pushes past three people in the line to chase the thing across the floor.

"Just two coffees. Mediums. Double double," I tell the server. I grab the coffees and throw a handful of change at him.

"Aha!" Mom twirls the tampon between her fingers. The cotton bulges out of the plastic wrapping.

"Mom!" I grab it from her and shove it in my pocket. I hold out the cardboard tray with the coffee. "Here."

She takes a cup and sniffs the lid. "I wanted hot chocolate."

I stare at her.

"You know too much caffeine makes me hyper."

Instead of walking, Mom insists we go back and get the car. Then drives at about ten kilometers an hour. Going slow saves gas, she says. She tells me to shut up when I try to tell her it's also illegal and unsafe.

A misspelled *Vacancys* sign is propped up in the grimy motel-office window. Half of the asphalt in the parking lot has buckled. A broken metal chair sits next to a garbage bin. "This looks promising."

Mom ignores my sarcasm. "Go see if they have a room."

I leave her peering through the windshield at me as I head inside. The office is dark and musty-smelling. The rattle of TV laughter drifts in from a back room. "Hello!" I call.

A huge jade plant takes up most of the counter. Next to it sits a plaid ashtray overflowing with butts. I yell louder. "Hello!"

The man who pushes through the bead curtain is wearing a sleeveless T-shirt that may have been white once. His suspenders part over his big belly. "Looking for a room?"

I roll my eyes. No. I'm the photographer from *Architectural Digest*. "For two."

He looks me up and down. "Better be an adult. I don't rent to kids."

I back away from his smell of cigarette smoke and what could be pork and beans. "It's me and my mom. She will want to look at the room first."

"Sure." He grabs a bunch of keys from under the counter, lifts a flap and shuffles through. His plastic slips-ons remind me of Grand's slippers.

Mom gets out of the car, and I get back in. It always makes me cringe to hear the stories she pulls out in these situations. Anything to save a buck or two. Or earn sympathy. Although she may really believe that we're on the run from an abusive husband who canceled her bank account. Or that we lost everything we own in a house fire.

It could be that she just watches too many daytime TV shows.

"He says he could shave off a hundred bucks if we stay the week," she tells me when she gets back. As if we've stayed that long in one place for years.

Weeks go by when we sleep more nights in the car than in a bed.

She slides back behind the wheel. "He offered to give me a break if I help out by doing some cleaning."

I laugh.

"I am quite capable, you know. Come on. Let's go check it out."

By the time I've cleaned out the wrappers and cans from the car floor and shoved my stuff in my bag, Mom is already sprawled on the bed, holding the TV remote. "Looks like they've got a decent cable package." On the Shopping Channel, a woman with makeup as thick as icing is pitching a huge purse. "Wonder if it comes in other colors," says Mom.

The furnishings include twin beds with mismatched covers, a white patio table between them, and a recliner with a worn-out seat. The TV's on a long arm attached to the wall. Inside the closet I find a rail with three metal hangers and a grubby bar fridge. The icebox flap is broken off. In the door is a strawberry yogurt.

Mom shrieks when it hits the metal garbage can. "What are you doing?"

"Cleaning out the fridge."

"Do it quietly." Mom lines up a row of vitamin bottles on the table. I have given up telling her that if she takes too many, she will only pee the extra vitamins away. She'll just show me where it says *All Natural* on the bottle. As if that explains everything.

"You need to take your meds," I tell her.

"At bedtime. This is just a nap. See if there's a glass or something in the bathroom."

She could start her housekeeping gig in there. A layer of scum lines the sink. A sliver of soap is stuck to the counter. The shower curtain has lost half of its rings.

At least the water runs hot. But there's no glass. "You'll have to drink from the tap," I call.

But she has already dozed off again. I grab my backpack and start to creep through the room. Then I stop and ease her purse from the foot of her bed.

Not quietly enough.

"What are you doing?" She squints at me.

"Checking to see if your other pills are here." *And looking for a lottery ticket I don't believe exists*, I don't say out loud.

"Quit nagging. You're not my mother." Mom grabs her purse, shoves it under the pillow and pulls the bedspread higher over her legs.

"I'm going out," I tell her.

"Don't be late," she mumbles.

Late for what?

Chapter Five

After a half hour of wandering, I find myself on a busy street. The traffic pulses past, fumes gusting into the air as cars slow down at the lights.

I duck into a corner store. Rusting bars on the doors and windows make the place look like a prison. Inside, one wall is plastered with cell-phone ads, all in Chinese. A tall kid with his baseball cap on backward leans on the counter. His jeans hang so low that his underwear balloons over the waistband. It's like looking at an accident. Gross. But hard to keep my eyes off.

"What are you staring at?" A girl—whoops, his girlfriend, I guess—glares at me. Her eyes are rimmed with black liner. Her dyed gray-blond hair stands up in all directions.

"Nothing. "

The guy turns on me. "Do we know you?" He looks at the girl. "Do we know her?"

"I dunno. Do you go to Henry Blackwell?" she asks me.

I guess that's her school. "No."

"I don't know you. So quit eyeing my boyfriend."

"I wasn't."

"Can I help you?" the woman behind the counter interrupts. "You go now, Dylan. See you tomorrow, Mara."

The girl and her boyfriend glance at the woman and then push past me to head out the door.

"They no trouble," the woman tells me. "I know them, so they no trouble for me."

"Okay." At least Mom isn't here. She would have started a fight right here between the canned spaghetti and toilet paper.

"Can I help you?" the woman asks me.

"How much are they?" I point at the box of individually wrapped cookies on the counter. Oatmeal with chocolate chips. Or maybe they're raisins. Though, by the state of this place, they could be flies.

"Forty-five cents. Three for one dollar."

I dig some change from my pocket. "Would you take seventy-five cents for two?" It's a habit. Bargaining for almost everything. One that makes me squirm a lot of the time. But also gives me a buzz when I pull it off.

She nods without giving it a second thought. "You take three. And I got milk day old." She looks toward the grimy cooler. "Milk and cookies very nice. Even better if milk free." She grins at me.

I grab one of the two cartons with an orange twenty-five-cent sticker, close the cooler door and thank her on my way out.

I check that Mara and Dylan aren't still around. It's easier to be anonymous in big cities. In smaller places, strangers stick out. I've been heckled, pushed around and beaten on by neighborhood bullies more times than my mother has missed doctor's appointments.

But there are only a teen mom pushing a stroller and a woman hauling a huge red-and-blue-striped bag. She could just be shopping, or maybe she's virtually homeless too.

I stay out as long as I can, wandering the streets, keeping my head down. It's almost dark by the time I get back to the motel. The neon sign flickers on and off, sending weird shadows across the parking lot.

Inside our room, I grope for the lamp switch. Mom is fast asleep. She mutters something and turns away from the light. She's still fully dressed, with her jacket around her shoulders and the covers slipping off her legs. She rarely gets right under the covers. Wary of bed bugs, she says.

One shoe is upside down on the floor, the other still on her foot.

I straighten her covers and put a cookie on the table next to her. I kick off my runners and prop up the pillows on my bed. I stretch out and lean against the headboard.

I watch Mom's chest rise and fall. I've spent hours doing this, in one badly lit room after another. It amazes me that her heart and lungs ignore the mess in her head. Her chest rises. Her chest falls. Over and over, one breath follows the other. Sometimes I count her breaths until I fall sleep. And when I wake up, I check again to make sure she's still breathing.

Most of the time I live in fear of her dying on me. The rest of the time I wish she would disappear.

Thinking like this always rattles me. And once I get stuck on thinking about all this stuff, I feel like a gerbil on a hamster wheel, going round and round and round with no way off.

I head into the bathroom. Hot water gasps and sputters out when I turn on the bathtub taps. I strip and lay my clothes on the toilet-seat lid. I make sure there is a towel on the rail, flick the knob to turn on the shower and step in.

Only a trickle comes out of the showerhead. The rest spurts from the tap and out of the tub. "Crap!" I bundle myself in the towel, leap out of the tub and drag my clothes back on without bothering to look for clean underwear.

It's been ages since we've been anywhere long enough to do laundry. I may have grown up with thrift-store clothes, but I draw the line at wearing cast-off underwear.

In big department stores, I wander through the fashion departments, trying to imagine myself with new clothes. Grand will foot the bill for lots of things, but clothes are hardly on his radar. While I'm there, it's not hard to stuff a couple of pairs of undies into my jacket sleeve or down my jeans.

When I come out of the bathroom, Mom's purse is still wedged under her pillow.

Maybe the lottery ticket is in her jacket. She's too out of it to notice me taking it off the bed. I'll be very careful and slow—

"What?" Her flailing hand catches the side of my chin. The impact wakes her. She hauls herself up.

"Shh, Mom. Go back to sleep."

"What you doing?" Her voice is thick.

"I tried to have a shower. It doesn't work."

"I'd like a bath." She struggles off the bed, mumbling, "It's cold in here."

While she is in the bathroom, I find enough tissues in her pockets to carry the bubonic plague. I dump them in the garbage. Her duffel bag holds a sweater, three stained T-shirts and a pair of pants that are too long.

Poor people give themselves away without even opening their wallets. Ill-fitting clothes that aren't washed often do it every time.

I'm trying to figure out where that ticket might be—if it really exists—when I almost trip on her shoe. I peer inside it. I notice the crease in the sole. I peel it back.

Would you look at this? The ticket! Not that finding it makes Mom any less crazy.

I'm trying to make some sense of the numbers—7-11-23-29-37-49—when she comes back into the room. "Give me that!"

I hold the ticket out of reach. "We should get it checked out."

"I did already."

"Worth millions?" I study the numbers again.

"Maybe not millions. But a lot."

"How much of a lot? By the way, you might want to do up your pants."

As she checks her fly, I jam the ticket in my pocket. When she looks up again, I pretend to be straightening the sole of

the shoe. I hand it to her. "Put this on.
The carpet's probably not been cleaned
in years. I see you changed your mind
about the bath."

"I'm hungry. Let's go find a sub or
something." She slips on her shoe, then
frowns at her other bare foot.

"In the bathroom maybe?" I say.

As soon as she leaves the room, I
tuck the lottery ticket deeper into my
pocket. It's probably worth nothing. But
just in case.

Chapter Six

We spend the evening sharing a foot-long sub and watching reruns with the lights out. I study Mom's eager face in the flickering light as she devours everyone else's funny lives, which hardly get a laugh out of me.

Next day, she's awake before me. I doubt she has even washed her face. But she is wearing more blush than a clown. If you can spot poor people at a hundred meters by their clothes, it is crazy women's makeup that gives them away. "You've overdone it a bit, Mom." I hand her a tissue when I come back out of the bathroom.

Do I try to make her look normal for her sake? Or mine?

She takes the tissue from me, frowns at it, then stuffs it in her pocket. "What would you like to do today?"

Sounds strange coming from her lips. *The zoo? A wander through the mall? A movie?* That's what any kid in a normal family might answer. Me, I hand her a breakfast bar from the emergency stash in my bag. "Have something to eat. Then take your pills, and we'll go find coffee."

She swallows a handful before I can check what she's taken, slurping water from the bathroom tap. Then she starts on the routine with her supplements.

She holds out a handful of tiny white pills. "Vitamin D is good for your bones. Improves mood too."

"There's nothing wrong with my mood." I break an apple in half and give her a piece.

"Maybe I'll stay here." She puts the apple on the bedside table and stretches out on the bed again. "It's raining."

"How can you tell? You haven't been outside for hours."

"Ever heard of the Weather Channel?"

I pull back one of the drapes. "It's not raining. And we need groceries. Proper food for a change." I hold out her jacket. "Put this on."

"You said it wasn't raining."

"Do it for me, would you? It will be cold, even if it's not raining." I sound like a kindergarten teacher.

She shrugs it on and hauls her purse over her shoulder. "Let's go, then, if we're going."

I herd her out of the room and lock the door behind us. "We need gas," she says as we walk past the car. "We'll get cash on the way. When's the check due?"

"There's enough in the account for the next few days anyway."

She never reads the receipts when we withdraw cash.

"We'll tighten our belts, that's what we'll do," she says cheerfully. "Come on then. Show me this park you told me about."

When we get there, Mom looks around happily as she settles onto the bench. I hand her half of the apple and listen to her take one bite at a time, chew for a bit, then spit out the skin into her hand.

"You think you can climb that?" She nods toward the jungle gym.

"I could. But I don't want to."

"Go on."

"No, Mom. I don't want to."

"Always such a wuss. Other kids? They play lacrosse. Do gymnastics. You just spend your life at the library. Go on. Or maybe you're afraid of heights."

"You climb it."

"All right. I will." She flicks her apple core onto the grass.

I pick it up and dump it in the over-flowing garbage can. "I didn't mean it!"

Instead of taking it one rung at a time from the outside, she crawls into the middle and grabs the highest bar. "Have to warm up before I take this on," she tells me, as if she's about to climb Everest.

"Okay. Okay. I'll show you how it's done." I clamber up the bars from the outside. "You going to join me?" I ask from the top. I am already regretting playing her crazy game.

Mom wiggles through, until she's sitting hunched next to me. "This is cozy."

"Not the word I would use." The bars are hard on my skinny butt.

When I see a woman walking her dog toward us, I'm off in seconds. "Come on down now."

"I like it up here," says Mom.

"Come on. Please."

The woman is closer now. More interested in us than in her dog.

"Mom!"

"What?"

"There's probably some rule about kids only on this stuff."

"Do you see a sign?" She looks around.

There is no sign. But the woman is getting closer by the second.

"Good morning!" Mom sings out.

"Good morning," the dog walker calls back. "The number of times I've been tempted to give that a try!"

I sigh a breath of relief.

"You'd have to lose a few pounds first," Mom tells her. "Thirty, maybe, if you plan to make it up here."

My stomach clenches. "Mom!"

The woman goes red and totters off without looking back.

"What?" Mom peers down at me. "What did I do?"

I stare at her.

"Well?"

I shake my head. "Nothing, Mom. Absolutely nothing." I give her a hand down. "Let's just sit here for a bit."

It's a quiet morning, almost peaceful. Three crows cackle at each other in a tree nearby. A small man with a big dog wanders across the other side of the park without looking our way. "Did you ever have a pet?" I ask, thinking of Jake and Bandit.

"A cat that got run over outside our house. Don't even remember its name." Mom frowns. "My mother…" She looks at me as if she expects me to finish her sentence. "She…" Mom frowns again.

Shakes her head. "Dad took care of it when he came home."

"What did your mother do?"

She glances at me, then away. "Nothing. She didn't do anything."

"You started to say…"

"I don't remember. Anyway, I've told you often enough. We can't have a dog until you're old enough to take care of it." It's funny how normal things sound crazy when they come out of my mother's mouth.

"I thought I would go over to the library." I stand up.

"I'm headed back. My shows come on soon."

I should persuade her to come. Anything to get her out of that grim motel. But Jake might be there. "Sure you're okay?"

"We've paid for the room. Might as well use it," she says. "You get the groceries, would you?" She scrabbles in her purse and hands me her bank card.

I don't really need it. That's something else she doesn't know. *Let it be our secret*, Grand said when he slipped me my own card. *It might be useful sometimes.* Who was the adult here? Her or me? Talk about blurred lines.

"Do you remember the way back?" I ask.

"I'm not a child. If I get lost, I can ask," Mom says. She frowns at me. "What's the name of our motel again?"

I'd like to think she's making a joke. I know she's not.

Chapter Seven

I skulk around the library for a while, hoping to run into Jake, trying not to look too obvious. Both computers are busy. So I settle down with the *Architectural Digest*.

I'm wondering who looks after the fancy fountain in front of Rod Stewart's mansion when someone nudges my foot. I try to quash the jolt of pleasure when I see Jake. "We meet again," he says.

"Hi."

"How's things?"

"Good." Now that he's here, I can't think of a single thing to say.

"I thought you might show up," Jake says.

"You did?" To distract myself from the heat rising in my face, I check the front of his jacket. "No ferret?"

"Bandit's at home with a cold."

"You kidding me?"

He grins. "You could say." He holds out a plastic bag. "Libraries are one thing. But I can't take him into the grocery store. Anyway. He needs his sleep. Ferrets are supposed to be nocturnal, though he can't tell time. But I'm headed home now. You could come and visit. I know he misses you."

"Right."

"Actually, he hardly knows you. So why not come and get better acquainted?" He's the one blushing now. I like how it brightens his pale face. He looks toward the computers. "Or maybe you're waiting your turn."

"I'm good."

He leans forward. "My mom's home. You'll be quite safe."

"Oh. I know. I mean…"

"I have kettle corn." He shakes the bag.

"Well…can we stop somewhere on the way?"

"Sure. What do you need to do?"

I show him the ticket. "My mom says it's a winner. Thought I could check this out." I shrug, as if it's a totally normal thing to do. As if it really doesn't matter to me.

Before he can answer, my phone rings. "Hello."

"Good morning, pet. How are you? Your mom there?"

"She's at home. In our room. I'm at the library."

"Ah, yes."

Jake pokes me in the back. "You can't use that in here." He points at the librarian watching us.

Outside, I lean against a huge cement planter that has been used as an ashtray.

"Everything okay there?" asks Grand.

I watch Jake through the window. "It's good."

"And your mom?"

"She's okay. What are you up to today?"

"Tidying up. Got Scrabble club here tonight."

He and I play sometimes. Mom too. But she makes up her own rules. And is a sore loser—no surprise there. "We haven't played for ages," I tell him.

He must hear the longing in my voice. "I miss you too, pet. But I'm glad things are okay. I worry. You know I do. You haven't even told me where you are." I hear him scrabbling for paper and pen.

"The Lion Motel. Richmond. I don't know the street."

"Richmond?" There's a pause. "She didn't go far this time."

Close enough for you to come and pick us up, I want to say. *To take us home.* "I'll get her to call you later." I swallow hard. "I miss you, Grand."

"Me too, pet. Me too."

He worries. I know he does. But not enough to take us in.

I'm shaking my head at the phone when Jake joins me outside. "You all right?"

"Fine." I'm not about to explain that I'm almost homeless with a crazy mother while my grandfather is

57

worrying but not doing anything about it only a few miles away. I avoid looking at him and scan the area instead. "So. Which way to your house?"

"I thought you wanted to check that ticket."

"It can wait. Probably not worth the bother." All I want right now is to feel Bandit curled around my neck, sliding down my chest, warming my heart.

We go for a few blocks without talking before Jake breaks the awkward silence. "So tell me one good thing. From when you were a kid." He swings the bag at his side.

"Why?"

"Think of it as an icebreaker. It's something Dad asks when he gets home from a buying trip. To tell him three good things. Start with one."

One good thing? I watch a garbage truck thunder past, scraps of paper fluttering in the air in its wake. "Okay."

I take a deep breath. "I'm left-handed, right? I had so much trouble cutting, Mom got me a special pair of scissors." Heavens knows where, or how she even noticed. "And some newspaper." The memory is pulling me along. "First I cut big pieces. Then smaller and smaller ones. We were outside on the balcony." In the middle of the night? I remember this detail, but I don't mention it to Jake.

"I cut and cut. And soon there were flakes of paper everywhere. Like snow. It must have been windy out there. Mom grabbed some scissors and paper too. And we went crazy. Cutting. Laughing. Waving our arms around to make the paper snow fly."

Jake starts telling me how his dad once woke him in the middle of a snowy night to go tobogganing. But I'm hardly listening. Cutting paper is normal. But in the middle of night? On an apartment balcony? Laughing and littering.

That's something only crazy people would do.

Then another memory sneaks up on me, one I'm not about to share with anyone. When I was little, Mom would slip notes or pictures under my pillow. *There's a lovely dream waiting for you*, she would say. *Go to sleep, and it will find its way into your head.*

What kid wouldn't stay awake worrying about little figures worming their way into her skull? But what also kept me from falling asleep was knowing that as soon as I opened my eyes, Mom would demand to know what I had dreamed. If I couldn't remember, she would get mad. And if I made something up, she would tell me I was lying. Either way, she would reach under my pillow, grab the paper and tear it into little pieces.

I had no business stealing her dreams, she said. They were too good for me.

Tucking a dream under a kid's pillow is a nice thing to do. But getting mad when she doesn't dream what you want her to?

One good thing does not always lead to another, I want to tell Jake. But then I would have to explain what I mean. And I hardly know myself.

Chapter Eight

Jake's place looks like any middle-class house on a middle-class TV show. It's a split-level with pale yellow siding. The double garage has gray doors. There's even a basketball hoop fixed to a tree next to the driveway.

Jake presses a button on a remote, and the garage doors slide up. They must be soundproof. And smellproof.

Before they are even open halfway, I hear chittering and scrabbling. And am enveloped in the funky animal smell.

I follow him through a warren of cages big and small, some on the floor, others stacked on benches. "Rodents over here." He waves to his left. "Reptiles on the right. Birds in the back."

"And *Mustaelida*?"

He grins at me. "You've got a good memory. Bandit's over here." Under the window, a wide cage runs the length of the garage. The ferret nudges up against the mesh, nose poking out, eyes blinking. "See? He remembers you," Jake says.

"I doubt it. Can he come out?"

"Sure." Jake opens the cage door and hauls the ferret out by the scruff of its neck.

I take Bandit from him and bury my face in the ferret's fur. "Smells good."

"I gave him a bath. In case we had visitors."

I drape Bandit around my neck while Jake gives me a tour. Some animals peek out of their woodchip bedding. Others nudge their noses against Jake's fingers as he reaches through the mesh to scratch, tickle and fondle them. He's so patient with them. Ends up with a handful that he juggles as easily as if they were hacky sacks. He reminds me of the parents with little kids I see on the street and in coffee shops, juggling kids, wiping noses. Talking about them fondly.

He shows me the angora rabbits, all white fluff that fill the hutch like huge marshmallows. "Steph's favorites," Jake says. *The ones all the girls like*, I remember him saying.

While I am being peered at and poked and licked and nudged by tiny paws and wet noses, Jake asks, "You have pets?"

"No. My mom…we've never been anywhere long enough, I guess."

"How come?"

"Oh. Long story." I look around. "All this must be a lot of work."

"It is." Jake takes a binder from a shelf. "*In case the SPCA ever comes calling*, Dad says. To Mom it's just another homeschooling project." He flips the pages.

"You're homeschooled?" I ask.

"How else could I get to go to the library in the middle of the day to pick up chicks?" He blushes. "Just kidding," he quickly adds. "What about you?"

"What about me?"

"School?"

"We just moved. Haven't registered yet." It's the line I always use.

He nods in a way that looks like he doesn't believe me. "So. Do you want to come in for that popcorn? Meet Mom and Steph?"

"I should go home. But thanks for showing me this."

"Why don't you come back for supper? Dad's famous spaghetti every Thursday."

"I don't know…"

"Go on. And if you don't want to feel beholden, you can help me clean out a cage or two afterward." He looks around like the proud housekeeper my mother will never be. Me neither.

"Maybe."

"You don't have to decide right now." Jake hauls the garage door closed. "Just show up at six. Dad will be cool."

The invitation nags at me all day as Mom and I wander the streets. We browse through a huge fabric store where Mom spends ages looking through heavy pattern books. She has never picked up a needle and thread as far as I know. I'm the one who sews on buttons.

We visit the park again, then come back to the room to watch endless M*A*S*H* reruns. And contests with frantic chefs making inedible food out of stuff I've never heard of.

It is typical day in the life of Grace and Leni Bishop. We won't be starring in any reality show anytime soon.

I want to go to Jake's.

But he was probably just being polite.

If I go, I should take something.

He's not even cute.

I shouldn't leave Mom alone too long.

I do like the way he blushes, how his eyes flash when he's talking proudly about his furry and feathered charges.

I stare at Mom spread out on the bed, her eye shadow smudged, crumbs on her shirt.

I look away, disgusted and hating myself for feeling that way.

"What is wrong with you?" Mom asks as the credits roll on yet another episode of *The Golden Girls*.

I check my watch. It's twenty to six. "There's something I need to look up at the library."

"Go."

"You fine here?"

"Don't I look fine?"

She's hugging her purse like it's a favorite cat. In the mess on the end table next to her is the TV remote, a box of crackers and a row of pill and vitamin bottles.

She's got everything she needs. "Okay. If you're sure."

The cutlery rattles as Jake deals plates around the table like playing cards. Jake's sister, Stephanie, grins at me. "You like basketti?"

"Sure. I love it." If there's a sale, I can pick it up for a dollar a can.

"Here we go." Their dad plunks a huge bowl of pasta on the table. "And here's the sauce."

"Dad's secret recipe," Jake tells me.

This is so like an old TV show. Happy families at suppertime.

We each have a cloth napkin rolled up inside a little woven holder. I don't want to get mine dirty, so I don't use it. To avoid flicking sauce everywhere, I coil a single worm of the spaghetti around my fork at a time. But it still splatters.

"Spaghetti must be the most dangerous food on the planet." I guess Jake's dad says this to make me feel better. But everyone looks at me. They look away again when they see me blushing.

Dinner takes forever. There's salad with two kinds of dressing. I eat mine plain.

I don't want to flood my plate and feel like an even bigger fool. Butter from the garlic toast dribbles down my chin. When I wipe it off, I see Jake's mom watching me.

Everyone talks back and forth. Over and around me.

The food is wonderful. But I can't wait to get out of there. I'm trying to come up with an excuse to leave when Jake's mom asks, "So how's school, Leni?"

I purposely don't look at Jake.

"What's your favorite class?" asks Stephanie. "I like recess best."

I shrug. "I don't know. Math, I guess?" Keeping track of our money must count for something. "But I like English," I say. Just in case they quiz me on calculus or something.

Jake's dad pipes up, "Reading anything good these days?"

"Dad owns Miller's Books. Did I tell you that?" Jake says.

Crap! I try to think of a book, any book. Sometimes I swipe a novel from a library book-sale cart. But I never seem to be able to get through any of them. None of them have anything to do with my life.

"Jake is whipping through *To Kill a Mockingbird* right now," his mom chimes in.

"I love this sauce," I say. Anything to get us off the topic of school and reading lists. I gulp down my last bite of pasta. "I should go."

"What about dessert?" asks Steph. "It's chocolate-ripple ice cream."

"I'm allergic to chocolate." I stand up. "Thanks for dinner. But I have to get home."

Jake's dad looks at his mom, who looks at Jake.

"I'll see you out," he says.

"I'm fine." There's an uncomfortable silence as I leave the kitchen. I shove my feet into my shoes at the front door.

"Why did she leave before we're done?" I hear Stephanie say. "Everyone likes chocolate."

Tears are smarting my eyes. I feel stupid and lonely and jealous. Their house would never make *Better Homes and Gardens*. But everything looks so comfortable. Jake's parents are friendly and Stephanie is sweet.

They are such a normal family.

And I am such an outsider.

Chapter Nine

"Leni! Hang on a minute."

I break into a trot. But within seconds Jake overtakes me. He runs backward down the driveway, facing me. "Why did you leave like that?"

"Like I said. I'm allergic to chocolate. Just being in the same room with it, I could go into antiseptic shock." I read about it on Wikipedia a few days ago.

"My tongue would swell. I wouldn't be able to breathe—"

"Garbage!"

"I am allergic. To chocolate and celery and tapioca pudding. And red peppers and pineapple on pizza—"

"It's anaphylactic shock, by the way," Jake interrupts. "Not antiseptic." He turns to walk alongside me. "And I'm allergic to raisins and egg whites and squid and cheese that's been aged more than ten years and red M&M's."

"Now you're full of it," I tell him.

"So why *did* you leave in such a hurry?" He sits down on the bench at a bus stop to tie his runners. It's a miracle he didn't trip running backward like he did. "Dinner wasn't that bad, was it?" Jake asks. "Steph noticed we forgot to put out the cheese. Is that why you left? Because there was no parmesan for your pasta? Or maybe you're allergic to that too."

I can't help but smile.

He grins back. Then he gets serious. "Are you going to tell me?"

I look back toward his house. "You have no idea, do you?"

He frowns. "Idea about what?"

"About my life."

He shrugs. "What about it?

"Our spaghetti comes out of a tin or in a little frozen package. Right now we're staying in one room in a motel. Who knows where we'll be this time next week. I haven't been to school since…I don't know. Maybe four years? The last time I sat at a kitchen table to eat was at my grand-father's. I don't know how long ago. Mom talked back to the TV news the whole time. Grand ended up taking his dinner into the garage just to get some peace."

Jake is watching me carefully. "What are you saying?"

"That happy family stuff? Back there?" I nod toward his house. "You take it all for granted. Everyone around the table together. A nice meal. Chatty conversation. Parents who don't wig out every time someone cuts them off in the car or doesn't wrap their sub the right way."

Jake stands up and puts his hands in his pockets. "I'm sorry. I didn't realize—"

"Why should you? It's not your life. It's my life. Always on the run. With a crazy mother and no money and no idea when it is all going to change. Or end. Knowing that if it does end, it won't end well."

"What about your grandfather? Can't he help?"

"He worries. He really does."

"That's good, isn't it?"

Jake doesn't get it. And, really, why should he?

"If he worries, it means he cares," Jake says.

"Sure, he cares." It's true. I know that. "But he's not about to do anything about it." I slump onto the bench.

I haven't done anything either. I could have begged, pleaded, insisted that he take care of us. What have I been waiting for? For Mom to figure out what a mess she—we—have made of things?

There's not much chance of that happening.

Jake plucks at my arm. "Come on. The bus is coming."

"I'm not taking the bus."

"It's cold. Come on. Let's take a ride."

"Where are we going?"

He pulls his chin back to his chest as if I've said the stupidest thing ever. "Is there somewhere else you need to be right now?"

So we ride the bus, and I tell him everything, or as much as I have the stomach to tell. The more I tell him, the quieter he gets. He does not look out of the window once while I tell him about Mom's pills and her moods and all the things she has been afraid of and all the reasons she gives me for moving from one place to the next and how hard it is to never make a friend.

I don't know the last time I ever told anyone this. If I ever have.

I tell him about the room we rented with the damp creeping up the wall. And the motel with so much dog hair in the carpet I could weave my fingers in it and pull it away in hanks. And the landlord I punched when he squeezed me against the wall in the hall one day to feel me up.

The more I talk, the more intently he listens.

"Doesn't sound like any fun." His voice is quiet.

He could say what a rotten mother Mom is. Then I'd have to defend her.

He could ask what we live on. And I would have to explain that if we didn't use Grand's address, we'd not even get welfare.

He could tell me that a diet of subway sandwiches and donuts is not good for a person. And I could ask him how anyone can eat decently with no way to cook real food.

But he only asks, "Do you think this is the way it will always be?"

I swallow hard. Put one hand in my pocket and finger the little piece of paper. "Mom figures that lottery ticket is the answer to everything. As if. It's just another of her crazy delusions."

When Jake puts an arm around my shoulders, I let myself lean against him. "It sounds awful," he says. He smells of straw and wood chippings and ferret. Of all those creatures he takes care of.

79

I lean against him for as long as I dare. When I pull away, he leaves his arm draped lightly over my shoulder. "Can't your grandfather help at all?" he asks.

"I told you. He worries. But it's just words."

"Someone has to be the grown-up. Take care of things," says Jake. "It shouldn't have to be you."

I've thought that a hundred times, but it sounds different coming from someone else. "You're right." I hear how quiet my voice is. So I say it louder. "I know. You're right." I stand, push past Jake and head down the bus aisle.

"Where are you going?"

"I'm going to call my grandfather."

Jake holds my hand as we wait for the bus to stop. Then we jump down onto the sidewalk.

I pull my phone out of my pocket, flip it open, then close it again. "I need to call Grand." I look around. "But not here. I should go back to our room."

"Where are you staying?" he asks. "You didn't say."

"The Lion Motel."

His eyebrows shoot up. "Jeez."

"What?"

He looks at his feet. "Nothing. It's just…well, I hear it's—"

"A dive?"

"Okay. A dive. I've heard all kinds of stuff. I'll walk you."

"You go home." I may have told him everything. Or most of it. But that didn't mean I wanted him to see Mom asleep in our grimy room with the Shopping Channel blaring in the background.

"Will you call me? Let me know what your grandfather says?"

"Sure."

When I don't move, he says, "You need my number."

"Oh. Sure."

He reels it off, and I punch it into my Contacts. *Jake* comes between *Grand* and *M Dr*. Three numbers are all I have in my phone. That's one more than I had yesterday.

It's a small thing. A good thing. "I'll call you."

As I head back, I catch myself practicing aloud what I will say to Grand. No one messes with a crazy person talking to themselves in the dark.

But I shut my mouth and keep on walking.

Chapter Ten

"Everything okay?" The motel manager ducks out of the office as I pass.

"You scared me!"

"Thought maybe you'd done a moonlight."

I look toward our room. The car's gone. But light shines between the closed drapes.

"Your mom left a while back," he tells me. "Seemed a bit upset."

"Upset how?"

"I heard yelling. In a real hurry she was, when she left."

She could have been shouting at the weatherman or a game-show host. "I'm sure she's fine," I tell him. Then I ask, "How did you know this?"

"I keep an eye out. Many people who come here, they are, well…" He looks around.

"Are what?"

"I could tell your mom was—"

"Nuts? My mom *is* nuts. As you have obviously noticed."

He frowns. "That's a bit harsh. She did seem a bit erratic."

Erratic is right. "Is there anything else?" Most of the time, I feel like I can't cope with my mother. But when anyone else notices? All I feel is their judgment.

Of her. And me. I should be able to control her, I hear them thinking. "Look. I better go."

"Of course. You go," he says. "And I'm sorry."

"It's okay. You mean well," I say. It's probably true.

"I mean for scaring you like that." He smiles gently.

My gut twists every time I come back to a dark, empty place. It's as if Mom leaves something dark and toxic behind her.

There's no sign of her. But the TV is blaring and the bathroom light is on.

I avoid looking toward the office as I head out again.

If there's one thing Mom likes better than a playground, it's a playground at night. I make the rounds, but the place is empty. Everything is in shadow. A swing creaks in a breeze. A piece of paper rattles across the ground. I sit down on the bench, pull my zipper up to my chin and shove my hands into my pockets. "Where are you, you silly cow?"

I'm talking to myself again. I clamp my mouth shut. But everyone does it, don't they?

When I scuff my feet on the ground, I discover a hole in my runners. I check under the bench to make sure Bandit's not on the loose. "What am I doing?" My laugh sounds crazy in the dark.

I bite the inside of my cheek until it hurts so much that tears fill my eyes. I try to swallow the feeling that I'm losing it. Any day it will be me yelling at servers at the coffee shop. Making rude remarks about people to their faces.

It's no wonder Grand always keeps us at arm's length.

On the street, a cop car slows down. I hold still until it moves off, its light smearing the dark.

I do another slow circuit of the playground, and then the community center. When I poke my head into the arena, all I see is a dad standing over his kid, yelling. I hear echoing voices, skates banging against boards, the hiss of skates on ice.

At Tim Hortons, the customers are all lit up in the windows. Even though I don't see Mom, I go in and ask for the washroom key. When the server in a dorky hairnet gives it to me right away, I tell him, "I changed my mind."

If the key's still here, my mother's not inside.

I feel him watching me as I leave. "Where can she be?" I ask myself.

A man stands aside to let me pass. "I'm sorry?" he says.

I don't answer.

She's done this before, taking off with no notice. Dozens of times. Sometimes for an hour. Sometimes for a whole day—or three. And when she gets back, she is mad, as if I am making a fuss over nothing.

When I run out of places to look for her, I head back to the room.

I plan to call Grand. I should call Grand. I had it all figured out, what I was going to say. *Someone has to be the grownup. And it can't be me.*

I think of how Jake moved between his furry and feathered creatures. Petting, stroking, murmuring. And how hard it is for me to touch my own bitter-smelling mother, to pick up after her, to hear her nighttime mumblings, her daytime rants.

Where *is* she?

I slump onto the bed and pull the covers over my head. The TV drones in the background. I wish I had something warm and soft to hang on to.

I don't know how much later I am startled awake by Mom looming over me. "Where is it? What did you do with it?"

"With what?" I squint up at her.

She whacks me with her shoe. "The ticket." She pulls off her other shoe. She bangs them together. "I was keeping it safe. You were the last person wearing my shoes—you know what I mean."

"Calm down."

"Where is my ticket?" Her cheeks are flushed.

"It's somewhere safe."

She yanks the bedspread so hard I hear it rip. "I went to claim the winnings. You made me look like a real jerk. I emptied my whole purse. Then I remembered it wasn't there. You should have heard the guy. Just because I took off my shoe—"

"Please don't tell me you hit him."

"Why would I hit anyone?"

"You just hit me."

"You deserved it. I checked both shoes. No ticket. Where is it?"

I can imagine the scene. Mom dumping the contents of her purse on the counter. Adding her shoes to the pile. Ranting and raving while the poor store clerk edges away, reaching for the phone, a panic button.

I guess it wasn't that store where the lady was so nice to me. The way she managed those two kids, she could have handled my mother. I pull myself up against the headboard. "So what happened?"

"When?"

"After you took off your shoes?"

"I put them right back on again. It's cold out, in case you haven't noticed."

"I mean, in the store?"

She waves a hand in the air. "They said they would call the cops. For what? It's a crime to take your shoes off?"

"Did the police come?"

"I passed a squad car on my way back here. But nothing to do with me." She drops into the armchair, mumbling to herself now. "I remember putting it in my shoe. Maybe another shoe. Another pair."

I don't bother to point out that she doesn't have another pair.

"If someone else finds that ticket, they will be living the high life while we—" Mom looks around. Suddenly her voice evens out, as if we were having a completely normal conversation. "Have you had supper? I'm starving."

"Have you taken your pills?"

"Why are you asking me that now?"

"You're acting like someone who is behind on their pills."

"I have to take them with food. You know that. You coming to find supper, or what?"

She doesn't give me time to tell her about supper at Jake's or to follow.

She's forgotten about the ticket. Again. There are benefits to having a mother with the attention span of a flea.

I stand at the door, staring into the night. The motel sign swings in the dark. A shadow of something—a cat, a rat, a ferret?—streaks along the sidewalk opposite me.

I half-expect Jake to appear in the dark.

Mom stalks past the car and across the motel forecourt without looking back. I step outside. Then duck back in. "Just go, then, why don't you," I mutter. "And don't come back."

Hours later, when I hear the door handle rattle, I stagger across the room.

"Jake!"

"Hi."

I'm aware of my crumpled clothes, my messy hair. The thick, stale taste in my mouth. "What time is it? How did you find me?"

He checks his watch. "Almost ten. You told me where you were staying, remember?" He comes in and closes the door. He looks around. "You alone?"

I look around.

Yes. I am alone.

I slump onto the bed.

He comes closer. Stands so close I feel the warmth from his legs on my knees. "What's wrong?"

When tears fill my eyes, I look away. "If you must know, my mom's gone." I bite my lip to stop my chin from trembling.

"Gone?"

"She left." My phone buzzes from somewhere under the covers.

"You going to get that?" he asks.

I stare the bed into silence. Grab the phone from under the covers and shove it in my pocket.

I will talk to Grand soon. I will make him listen. Make him do something more than just worry.

But right now… "Will you help me find my mother?" It is so hard to ask.

"Sure." And it seems so easy for Jake to answer.

Chapter Eleven

"The park?" says Jake. "Sure. If you say so."

He waits while I brush my hair and change my shirt before we head out. I feel groggy after oversleeping. And a lump sits right in the middle of my chest. It could be hunger. Resentment at all the garbage my mother puts me through.

Or just the same old fear that has been lodged there for years.

But it helps to have Jake walking next to me, taking a detour behind the mini mall, ducking into the Laundromat. He checks with me when he sees people who could be her but aren't. Others who could only be my mother in another lifetime in which she ate well, had a decent place to live and stuck to her meds.

When we get to the park, Jake takes a detour to help a kid struggling with a bike that's much too big for him. He's always taking care of someone, it seems.

"There she is," I tell him with relief. "That's her."

"Where?"

Mom is crouched on the top of the jungle gym, surrounded by three kids about my age. I can't hear what they are saying. But I don't like the way they are all standing around, staring up at her. "Leave her alone!" I sprint toward them, Jake at my side.

The one girl in the group turns toward me. "You can just butt out." She pulls back and frowns at me. "Hey! I know you."

She's the one from the corner store. And her boyfriend is with her. His pants are hitched up a bit higher today.

When all three of them turn toward us, my mother lobs a shoe at them. It hits Dylan in the back. "Hey!" He grabs a bar as if he's about to leap at her.

Jake hauls him away by his jacket. "Forget it!"

The other boy takes a step toward Jake. Points. "I know you."

"Mattie, isn't it?" Jake nods at him. "From Boy Scouts, right? Or was it Cubs?"

The kid's face goes bright red.

"Mattie? Cubs?" Dylan smirks.

"It's Matt, actually," he tells Jake. His eyes blaze. "That was a long time ago. When you were a teeny, tiny shrimp," he says. "Oh. And look at you. Still a shrimp."

Jake simply stares at Matt, the glimmer of a smile on his face.

Mara snickers.

"I never knew you were a Boy Scout!" jeers Dylan.

"You never asked," Matt mutters.

Mara snorts again.

All this nonsense about Mattie the Boy Scout seems to fascinate my mother, who is watching them all. They step away as I sidle up to the jungle gym. "You okay, Mom? You coming down?"

She shakes her head.

"Come on."

"I like the view," says Mom. But she's still watching the three kids.

They glance at Jake, then skulk off.

"I've got your lottery ticket here." That will get her down.

"Show me."

"It's here somewhere." It's not in the first pocket. Nor the next.

Dylan, Matt and Mara are now headed back across the park, the two boys roughhousing as they go.

"Seems that Mattie didn't want to relive our Boy Scout days," Jake says.

"Who are you?" Mom asks him.

"This is Jake," I tell her. "A friend of mine."

"I don't want you dating boys I haven't met."

"We're not dating!" I say.

"Nice to meet you," Jake says to Mom, with no sign in his voice that there's anything strange about greeting a grown woman sitting on top of a jungle gym.

"So where's that ticket?" asks Mom from her perch.

"It's here somewhere." I find it tangled up with a tissue in a pocket I just checked. I hold it out to her.

"Give it to me!" Mom reaches for it.

"Watch out!" cries Jake.

It happens in a flash. And takes forever.

One minute Mom's up there, yelling at me. The next, she's leaning, pitching, banging against the bars as she topples, tumbles and lands in a heap.

I leap forward. Kneel at her side. "Mom. Mom." She's very still, her eyes closed. "Call an ambulance," I yell. "Someone, please." Her arm should not look like that.

"Don't move her." Jake pulls out his phone.

I pet Mom's face. Stroke her hair. Like she's one of Jake's menagerie. I cover her with my jacket.

It's ages before I hear the sirens. Damp creeps through the knees of my pants. Someone drops a coat across my shoulders.

A hand falls on my shoulder. "They're coming, Leni," says Jake.

The siren is louder now. Mom still hasn't moved.

The ambulance drives up, and the sirens stop. Two pairs of boots appear on either side of a set of wheels. "Come away, Leni." Jake pulls me up.

The men kneel on either side of Mom. Lean over her with stethoscopes, an arm cuff, an oxygen mask. They put splints on both sides of her head. Two on her arm.

"Is she okay?"

"We've got her," says the paramedic. "We'll just be a couple of minutes here. Then we'll take her in."

Mom's eyelids flicker. But her eyes don't open. Her skin is pale, almost blue. I grab her purse. Gather her fallen shoe. Take the other off her foot. I wish

I'd left the stupid ticket where I found it. It's probably not worth a dime.

I follow a paramedic as he climbs into the ambulance behind my mother. "Where are we going?" He is too busy to answer.

Just as the doors are about to close, I lean down to Jake. "Here. Take this." The lottery ticket is damp from being clenched in my hand the whole time. "I never want to see it again."

My mother lies as still and cold as stone.

I think of Jake's animals. The warm, funky smell of litter, spilled water, warm fur.

The binder thick with everything he knows about them. Everything he does for them.

He can take care of thirty-two animals. I can't even look after one person. Not anymore.

Chapter Twelve

I rehearse everything I plan to say to Grand as the paramedics wheel Mom through Emergency. They direct me to a seat against a wall. They wheel her into a cubicle and pull the rattling curtains closed. A nurse hurries in, then a doctor. I am still rehearsing my speech to Grand when the paramedics leave, giving me a quick pat on the shoulder as they pass.

More people hurry back and forth. A phone rings. A baby cries. Someone moans. Equipment ticks and hisses and whines.

As I finally pull out my phone, a passing nurse says, "Please make your call in the waiting room."

I go through the swinging doors and stand in front of the candy machine. After I punch in Grand's number, I wait through eight rings. I'm about to hang up when he answers.

"Yes."

"It's me."

"I thought you were going to get your mom to call me."

"She's in hospital."

"In hospital? What happened? Is she going to be all right?"

"That's a stupid question."

He pulls in a breath. He's wheezing. Of course he's wheezing. Who wouldn't be, smoking more than a pack a day?

"I'm sorry. But it is a stupid question. She fell off a jungle gym, if you must know. A jungle gym! She's broken her elbow or something. And has a concussion. Of course she's not going to be all right. At least, not for a while. Maybe never. How do I know? I don't know anything. But I know *I'm* not going to be all right. Maybe you don't know that mental illness can be genetic—"

When I see all the faces looking my way, I turn my back on them and hold the phone close. "Right now, I know that I *will* go crazy if someone else doesn't take care of her." I slide down the wall till my butt hits the cold, shiny floor. "I can't do it anymore, Grand." I keep my voice as steady and calm as I can. "Think of Mom. As your kid, I mean. Not as a grown-up. Think of her as someone who needs more than clothes and food and shelter. Who needs someone to take over. Take charge. Take notice—"

"Leni…"

"Take an interest. Take steps. Take a moment, just one teeny-tiny moment, to look at her and see what's going on with her. And with me."

"Leni!"

"What?" I guess I'm yelling. A baby lets out a shriek. I smile an apology at its mother. "What?" I ask Grand more quietly.

"Hang on a minute. I need my hearing aid…" His voice fades.

Has he heard a single thing I've said? I drop my head to my knees. I could laugh. I could cry.

But I don't have the energy to do either.

"Pet? Are you still there?"

"Grand. Can you do something for me? Please."

"What is it?"

"Come and get me." I struggle to keep my voice from shaking. "Me and Mom.

Please come and get us." I sound like a six-year-old. "We need you."

I don't know what it was I expected. Arguments? A whole bunch of reasons and excuses? But there's only silence at the other of the phone. "Grand? Did you hear me?"

"I heard you perfectly well."

When I get back to Emergency, I find that they have moved Mom to a treatment room. I can hear her yelling through the door.

Grand said he'd come. As soon as he can. He may not have agreed to take us home. But he is coming.

I need to see it to believe it.

A woman wearing an ID badge edges past gurneys and IV poles. "Helen Bishop?" She looks at her clipboard, then back at me. "I'm Sarah Smales. A social worker here."

"Yes? And it's Leni."

"All right. Leni. I've been asked to talk to you about your mother. It seems she's a bit—" She studies her notes. Then looks up again as Mom yells.

"Get me out of here. Someone get me out of here. Where's Leni? Leni!"

I think I liked her better unconscious.

"I'll just take a quick look to see how things are going." The social worker knocks once, then goes into the room.

I sink back into the chair and rest my head against the wall. I sit up again when I hear footsteps. "Jake!"

"I thought you might like company." He digs the ferret out of his coat. Dumps him in my arms.

"You can't bring him in here!"

"I didn't see any sign saying *No ferrets allowed.*"

Bandit is twining himself around my neck, looking for a way into my sweater.

"Put him away," I tell Jake. "Before someone sees."

Jake takes Bandit from my neck and waits for him to settle into his jacket before he sits down. He tips his chair back against the wall. "That your mom?" He nods toward the door. "She going to be okay?"

"She broke her elbow. And has a concussion. But no. She's not going to be okay, if you mean is she going to suddenly become a model parent dedicated to the well-being of her child."

"Stupid question, I guess."

"I called Grand. He's on his way." I look around and blink—anything to keep the tears back. "I don't know what he'll do when he gets here. She'll still be crazy. I'll still be stuck with her. I don't know that it will change anything."

Chapter Thirteen

Jake leaps up and digs into the pocket of his jeans. "But this might. I checked out the ticket. Four numbers. She got four winning numbers."

I grab it. "You're kidding! You're sure?"

"Would I kid you?"

I turn the ticket over. Look at the numbers again. They still don't mean anything to me. "It really is a winner?"

"Yes. Four numbers. But it's maybe not the millions your mother told you…"

"That doesn't matter."

He hasn't heard me. "It's only $763 and change." He purses his lips and scrunches up his nose. "Sorry it isn't better news." His voice brightens. "But seven hundred bucks? There's a lot you can do with that. You must think so too."

Sure, there's a lot we could do with seven hundred bucks. Seventy, even. But that's not why I'm grinning. What do they say? It's not about the money?

"It's not about the money," I tell Jake.

"It's not?"

I wave the ticket in his face. "You don't get it. But why should you?" I laugh at the baffled look on his face. "Don't you see? She wasn't totally delusional. That's the point. Maybe she's not really as crazy as I think she is."

The words are hardly out of my mouth when the social worker comes back. "It's a serious break," she tells me. "Your mom needs surgery. She will be here overnight at least, so we've got to get you sorted out." She steers me away with a hand on my arm. "Let's go to my office."

"Jake…"

He is leaning against the wall, holding his chest.

The social worker stops. She looks at him, then back at me. "I'm sorry. Is he with you?"

Jake moves toward us. "Yes. I am with her."

I grin at him. He's with me.

"Can he come too?" I ask.

"I think we better deal with this in private, don't you?" says the social worker.

"But…" As I move closer to Jake, my elbow collides with his chest.

Bandit sticks his head out of Jake's jacket.

The social worker shrieks. She drops her clipboard.

Jake and I look at each other and burst out laughing.

Jake and Bandit are banished outside. I can't tell if the social worker is madder about the ferret or at Jake and me laughing.

But the look on her face was priceless. And it was the best laugh I've had in weeks.

In her cramped office, she talks over me every time I try to speak. "It seems that your mother needs more help than you can give her."

"I know that. I called—"

"We need to get hold of her medical records so we can devise a proper treatment plan. And we need to know her next of kin. When was the last time she saw a doctor?"

"She'll be okay. I can make sure she—"

"Your mother is having a psychotic episode, as far as I can tell. We'll know more when she sees the psychiatrist tomorrow. And we need to keep an eye on that concussion. So we're going to admit her to the ward."

"She doesn't like psychiatrists. The last one—"

"How about you let the professionals manage—"

"Let me finish! I know her. You don't. She doesn't need another fancy psychiatrist asking her more stupid questions that she can't answer. And then giving her prescriptions for more pills that will make her sleep, or hallucinate, or get into arguments. Don't you see?"

"What I see is a mother who needs more help than you alone can—" This time she's the one who is interrupted by a knock on the door. She frowns with impatience. "What *is* it?"

A nurse sticks her head into the room. "There's a gentleman here who says he's—"

"I can speak for myself." One pant leg droops over the top of his boot. His shirt is untucked. His hair is sticking up, and there are dark patches of stubble on his cheeks.

"Grand!" I leap up and hug him hard. Sure, I am pleased to see him. But I also want to protect him from the social worker's prying eyes. "You came."

"And about time, don't you think?" He stares at me for a moment, then turns to the social worker. "Now that I'm here, you can tell me what's going on."

She looks at her notes. "Mr. Kennett, I presume? Do sit down. Leni. How about you wait outside while your grandfather and I go over a few things?"

Grand grabs my hand. "This girl has brought things this far. She needs to know where we're going from here. Sit down, pet."

While words flow back and forth across the desk, I hold on to the arms of the chair in case I float away with relief.

Chapter Fourteen

Grand scrubs at his hair as he looks around the motel room.

I used to imagine living in an old Victorian house with fancy porches. In a sleek wood-and-glass house set in wide fields. Or in a loft conversion with high ceilings, and a bathtub in front of long windows. Now all I want is to be back in Grand's living room with its musty smell and fraying furniture. "It's no different or worse than anywhere else," I tell him.

He surveys the empty cracker boxes, the clutter of yogurt containers. "You eaten lately?" he asks.

"There's a Timmy's down the street."

I'll have a bacon-and-tomato sandwich. And a bowl of chili. And a muffin. An iced cappuccino. Maybe two of everything. I don't remember ever being this hungry.

"Remember my chili?" Grand asks when we're seated at a sticky table with our food in front of us.

"Sure." Now that I think of it, it's probably the only hot meal he has ever made from scratch. "With Yorkshire pudding."

"Your grandmother got me into that habit. But you wouldn't remember her." He stirs his chili. Asks me without looking up, "Does your mother ever talk about her?"

"She says I'm tall enough to be a dancer like Gran. And that I have her widow's peak." I touch my brow. "Not much else though."

"All true."

"What happened to her?"

He puts down his spoon. "You were so little. Three? Four?"

I shrug. He wants to talk about old times. I want to know what's going to happen from here on in. "I don't know."

"It had something to do with all the drugs she was on. Too much. The wrong combinations. There was an autopsy, of course." He dabs at his mouth with his handkerchief. Then his brow. "Nowadays they might call it an accidental overdose."

I feel a chill, picturing the medication bottles lined up beside my mother's bed. "What kind of drugs?"

"I don't remember their names now. So many at one time or another. Anti-psychotics."

Like Mom's.

My spoon clatters as I put it down. I wrap my arms around myself. I'm suddenly not hungry anymore. Mental illness is genetic. Everyone knows that.

"Your mom never told you?" he asks.

"That my grandmother was nuts too?"

"Leni!"

"Well, if she was taking those drugs, she must have been."

He looks at his bowl as if he is trying to figure out how it got there. Then he looks back at me. "You don't remember her at all?"

"Not really. Just smells. Lemon, I think. And licking cake batter out of a bowl. A nonsense song about mares and does."

He starts to hum something or other, then stops when he notices people staring. People probably thinking, *Crazy old man!*

Mom would get into a shouting match with them. For staring. For laughing. Not that she ever needs a reason. Fight or take flight, that's what Mom does. Two of the most basic instincts when humans are under stress.

Grand's cold hand reaches for mine. "We...I should have told you long ago." He looks tired. His eyes are watery, his lids red. "Your grandmother? The other Helen? Of course, you would know you were named after her. We married right out of high school. She was wild. Exciting. Tireless." He speaks with a mix of pride and sadness as he describes how she was also committed and driven. Dancing six, eight, ten hours a day. Dancing with bleeding feet and not enough sleep.

He uses donut holes as punctuation when the story gets too hard. Or when he forgets his place or the words just won't come. His shirtfront gets whiter and whiter with powdered sugar.

My chili is cold now. I can't touch my sandwich.

It is hard hearing about my grand-mother's breakdowns and recoveries, the friendships she blew, the fights she got into. "Things settled down for a bit when we had Grace," Grand tells me. "Helen was determined to do everything right. But that soon led to manic house-cleaning, overprotectiveness as Grace got bigger, confrontations at school."

I clench my jaws. This all sounds so familiar.

"Things were harder—and easier—when your mom got older and was busy with her friends and out of the house most of the time. And when your mom started to act up, get into trouble,

I assumed it was the usual teenage stuff. Rebelling against her difficult mother…all that. Though I probably knew on some level what was going on. I couldn't face it, I guess. I should have. All my time was spent taking care of Helen." He studies my face. "You didn't know any of this?"

I shake my head. I don't trust myself to speak.

"Then Grace met your dad. What was she? Seventeen? Eighteen." His gaze is focused on the past. Not me. "They moved away. I should have kept up with you both better, but I still had Helen to care for. Then your dad left. Your grandma died soon after. I saw a bit of your mom and you. But not enough. I guess I was aware that things weren't quite right. But the sicker your mom got, the less I could do."

He looks up at me, challenging, apologizing, "I should have done more.

I know. But I couldn't. I had nothing left." He drags a handkerchief from his pocket and dabs at his eyes.

"Me neither." It comes out as a whisper.

Grand leans forward as if he hasn't quite heard.

"Me neither, Grand," I tell him. "I can't do it anymore."

He takes a wheezy breath. He pulls himself up straight. He shakes his head slowly, staring at me. He reaches across the table, runs his palm down my face, flat-handed as if wiping away tears, dirt. "I know, pet. I know. But perhaps we can do it together."

I rest my cheek against his open palm. Feel the warmth against my cheek.

"Think we could give it a try?" he asks. "Bit of a dragon, that social worker. I've always tried to stay clear of them. But she did have ideas." He pulls out a sheet of paper. "Some resources that we could try. Groups for people like us. The ones taking care of those who can't take care of themselves. Seems there's more help out there than there was in your grandmother's day." He studies the notes for a moment. Then looks up at me. "So?" he asks. "What do you think?"

I take the paper from him. Scan it quickly.

He can't do it alone. Neither can I. But we'd have each other. And Mom would have us both. "Okay."

His mouth trembles as he smiles at me. "Good girl."

As we leave, he puts his arm around me. I inhale the familiar smell of motor oil. Dust and age. Nicotine. "You've got to quit smoking," I tell him. "I need you to be around for a long time. Mom and I both do."

"One thing at a time, pet. One thing at a time."

Chapter Fifteen

Jake shifts from foot to foot as Grand
settles Mom in our car.

"Where's Bandit?" I ask.

"He can't stand long goodbyes. You
don't have to go, you know." Jake nods
toward the car. "Your grandfather can
take care of her now."

I've spent the last few days alter-
nating between his house and my

mom's hospital room, where we played Scrabble and let her win. We watched endless reruns on the TV and shared submarine sandwiches. It was not much different than how Mom and I usually spend our time. But it felt different— better—with Grand there too.

"I do have to go," I tell Jake.

Grand closes the car door. A buddy gave him a ride to Richmond so he could drive us back. He started planning how to get us home as soon as he got my call.

"There's room for you at our place," says Jake. "And you could take classes with me."

"You asked your mom?"

"Sure." I can tell he's lying by the way he doesn't look me in the eye. "She said it would be cool."

"That's crap, and you know it," I tell him. "But thanks anyway."

Grand says the first thing we have to do when we get home is register in school. Wikipedia and *World Book* can only take a person so far, he says.

"I have to go," I tell Jake.

He nods slowly, like he knew that all along.

"You coming or not?" Grand is standing by the open passenger door, smoking.

"I can't live with my mom," I tell Jake. "But I can't live without her. How's that for a cliché?"

And Grand needs me as much as I need him. "But thanks."

"Will you call me sometimes?" When he puts his arms around me, I want to stay there so badly. Enclosed. Warm and safe.

"You've got ten seconds," Grand roars. "Then I'm leaving without you." He climbs into the car and closes the door.

I back away from Jake before I am tempted to hang on so tight I won't ever let go.

"Come back to visit," he says. "I'm not going anywhere."

I kiss his cheek. "Thanks for everything."

Jake has given me a third good thing. Somewhere to return to, after years of never staying in one place. And never having a reason to return.

I watch him watch us drive away.

Until we turn the corner. Then it's just me, Grand and Mom.

She mumbles something from the backseat. I can just see the top of her head and her bad arm sticking out from under the comforter. Between the driver's seat and mine is a white paper bag full of prescriptions. I have no idea what she needs to take when.

As if he reads my mind, Grand says, "Don't worry about a thing, pet. I've got all the instructions." He taps his chest. Maybe they are written on his heart. Or on a piece of paper in his inside pocket.

I grab my backpack from the floor. Dig out the lottery ticket. The numbers 7-11-23-29-37-49 still don't make any sense to me. Maybe they never did, not even to Mom. "Can you find a store?" I ask.

"Can't it wait?"

I know he hates driving. "Sure. When we get home will be soon enough." I lean over the seat to ease the ticket under Mom's comforter. She is fast asleep. Her eyes flutter as if there's a whole other story going on behind her lids. Which there probably is.

I just hope it has a happy ending.

ACKNOWLEDGMENTS

I am so proud to be part of the Orca "pod" and grateful for editor Melanie Jeffs' special insights into Leni's story.

Lois Peterson's books for children and youth have been published in various languages and nominated for awards in British Columbia, Ontario, Saskatchewan and Texas. A keen storyteller and writing instructor, Lois works for a large public library in BC, volunteers in the community, hikes, listens to music and spends the rest of her time reading almost anything she can get her hands on. Find out more about Lois's books and presentations at www.loispeterson.blog.com.

Titles in the Series

orca currents

orca *currents*

For more information on all the books
in the Orca Currents series, please visit
www.orcabook.com.